D0487532

CAVAN COUNTY LIBRARY
ACC No. C/284251
CLASS NO. JF/0-4
INVOICE NO. 10363 IES
PRICE £10.36

To my niece Sheri
and her ginger cat – Y.Z.

A TEMPLAR BOOK

First published in the UK in 2016 by Templar Publishing,
part of the Bonnier Publishing Group,
The Plaza, 535 King's Road, London, SW10 0SZ
www.templarco.co.uk
www.bonnierpublishing.com

Copyright © 2016 by Yuval Zommer

1 3 5 7 9 10 8 6 4 2

All rights reserved

ISBN 978-1-78370-575-7 (hardback)
ISBN 978-1-78370-576-4 (paperback)

Designed by Genevieve Webster
Edited by Alison Ritchie

Printed in China

ONE HUNDRED SAUSAGES

YUVAL ZOMMER

Cavan County Library
Withdrawn Stock

t templar publishing

CAVAN COUNTY LIBRARY

Scruff's favourite things in the whole wide world were
SAUSAGES!
Especially the ones in the butcher's window.

Wherever Scruff went (and he went everywhere),

SHOO!

he hoped that SAUSAGES were on the menu . . .

NO DOGS ALLOWED

Every night when Scruff fell asleep he dreamt of SAUSAGES: teeny ones, spicy ones, big fat juicy ones; curly ones, stinky ones and yummy, scrummy veggie ones!

One fine morning as Scruff stopped for his favourite daily
sniff at the butcher's: SHOCK! HORROR!
Every single top-notch sausage had been STOLEN!

The police chief and the butcher and the mayoress held an emergency meeting.
They had their eye on one prime suspect . . .

The very next day there were WANTED posters all over town.

"Woof! Double, triple woof!" gasped Scruff.

"I must sniff out the **real** culprit before I get into deep trouble!"

Scruff called out to his friends. "Everyone – HELP!
There's a thief on the loose. We need to catch him!"
"I only know how to catch sticks," whimpered Ada the Afghan.

"I can barely catch my breath . . ." huffed Percy the Pug.

"I only ever catch colds!" yapped Pixie the Poodle.

"I can't even catch my own tail!" sighed Sidney the Sausage Dog.

"Fine! I'll go and find the thief and **all the stolen sausages** on my own then," said Scruff.

"Did you say SAUSAGES?!" barked Scruff's friends excitedly. And soon they were all trying to think up dog-genious plans to catch the criminal.

Scruff's plan had three very important steps:

Percy thought he might charm the thief with his dashing good looks!

Ada always fancied herself as a bit of a detective.

Sidney suggested luring the thief with a cunning disguise.

Pixie was too busy filing her nails to think.

Scruff was about to give up, when he detected some **delicious** smells . . .

STATION

30

MUSTARD

WANTED
FOR SAUSAGE SNAFFLING

HAVE YOU SEEN
THIS DOG?

15

HOT DOG
WRAPPER

A sniffing party marched into town led by Scruff.
There were no signs of the sausage thief anywhere, but there
were plenty of rather SMELLY clues to investigate . . .

At last Scruff caught the **awesome** whiff of simply scrumptious sausages!
As the smell got stronger and stronger, Scruff began to dig

and dig and dig (digging was what Scruff did best). He dug under the wall,
and came out the other side, where right before his eyes was . . .

. . . the sausage-stealing culprit. Just as Vinnie's van
was zooming off to market, super-speedy Scruff managed to
grab hold of a string of top-notch, scrummy, stolen SAUSAGES!

He clung on for dear life as the van sped
along the road, until SMASH! CRUNCH!
it got stuck in a most inconvenient ditch
(dug by you-know-who!).

The sausage-thief was nabbed at last . . . Everyone cheered,
yapped and barked as Vinnie's final destination turned out to be
not the local market but the local police station.

The next day a very proud mayoress, a very grateful butcher
and a very impressed police chief presented Scruff with a special award . . .

a big gold rosette for Scruff the Wonder Dog,
the best crime-solving, sausage-sniffing, hole-digging dog in town!

To celebrate their triumph, Scruff and his four-legged friends
were treated to a slap-up meal at the town's top restaurant.

Can you guess what was on the menu?
Scrumptious, **succulent, sizzling SAUSAGES!**

Scruff was just about to get started on second helpings when . . .

. . . he discovered that Vinnie wasn't the only sausage-snaffler in town.

And as for Vinnie, he had to pay
a hefty fine and spend his Saturdays
stuffing sausages – teeny ones, spicy ones,
big fat juicy ones; curly ones, stinky ones
and yummy, scrummy veggie ones!

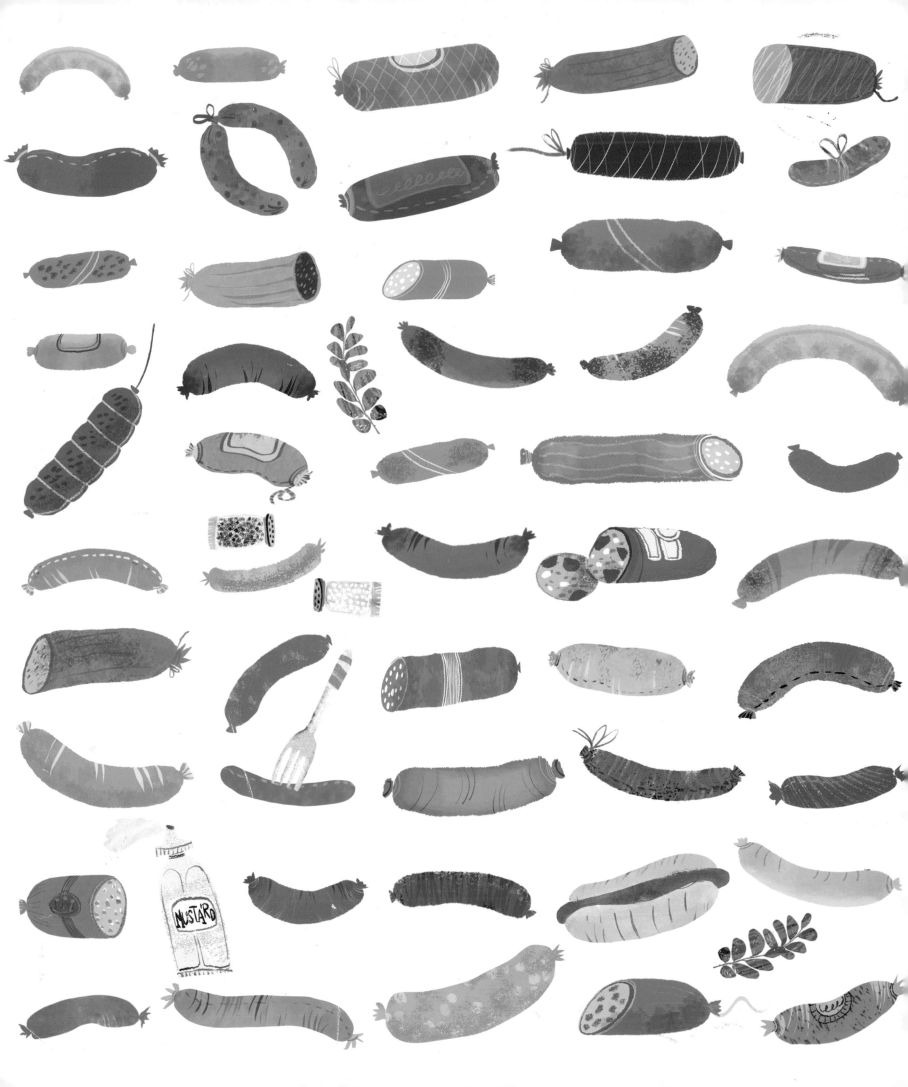